YEAR ONE
with
TYPE ONE

Written by Mike Suarez
Illustrated by Olsi Tola

It started with so many trips to the sink
where I'd fill up my cup and have lots to drink.

I felt tired and weak and was always thirsty.
On top of all that, I kept having to pee.

I drank too much water for such a small guy.
I went to the doctor to figure out why.

To check my blood sugar
I stuck out my finger.
I felt a quick poke
but it didn't linger.

I watched my mom chat
with my doctor and nurse
about heading to Boston
before things got worse.

Mom rushed to the Children's ER in Longwood.
Dad met us both there as fast as he could.

They connected my arm to a thin plastic tube.
I got nothing to eat but a plain old ice cube.

I waited twelve hours to actually eat
and four hours more to get up on my feet.

You might think that this place
would give me the creeps.
But I had some fun
staying here for three sleeps.

While Mom and Dad learned
how to give me my shots,
I relaxed with a book
of "Connect-the-Dots."

While I gave pretend shots to my stuffed blue bunny, my teenage roommate was being so funny.

Being stuck in one room was getting so boring
so Dad took me downstairs to do some exploring.

Butterflies on the big screen followed my motion
as I ran to a fish tank as wide as the ocean.

Each stair going up made a musical sound

while a giant Great Dane was just walking around.

After three nights away from my little sister,
I wanted to hug her and tell her I missed her.

This year's been a process, learning to cope.
Shot after shot. Poke after poke.

Belly, legs, arms... shots go any which way.
We spread them around, since they're six times a day.

Mom e-mails a log to the nurses each week.
They check if the carb ratios need a tweak.

Mom checks in at night
with a lamp on her head
sometimes with a juice box
to drink in my bed.

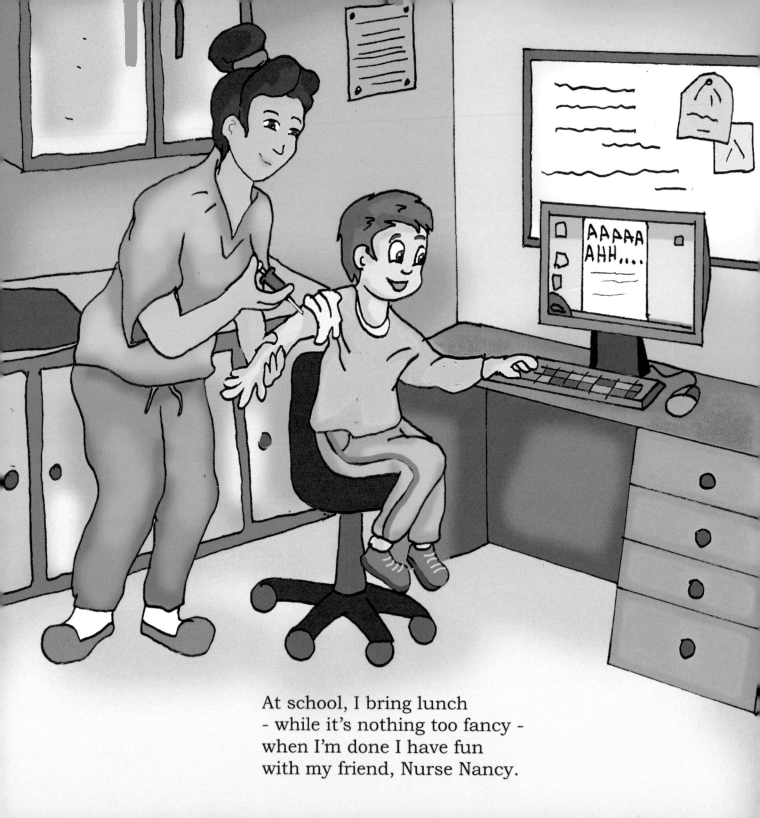

At school, I bring lunch
- while it's nothing too fancy -
when I'm done I have fun
with my friend, Nurse Nancy.

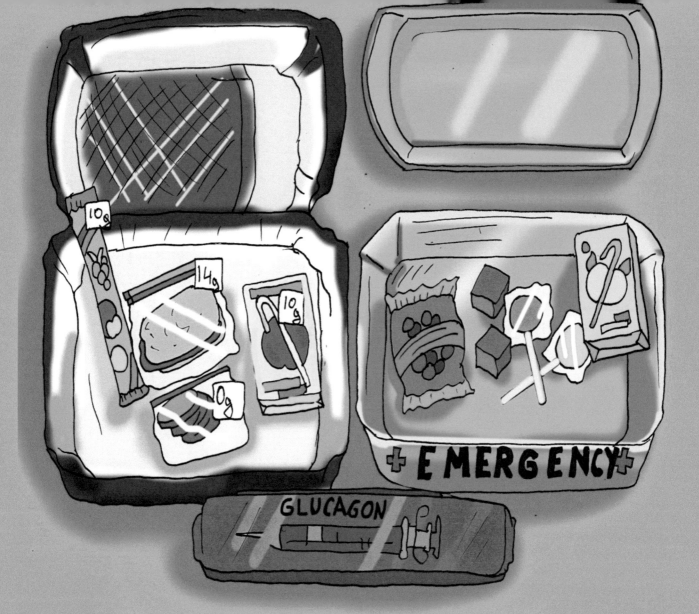

We count carbs to know what goes into my body.
But no sneaking snacks! That's beyond being naughty.

(Except when my blood sugar suddenly drops;
we can bring it back up with some green lollipops.

And if I can't eat when my sugar's too low
a shot of glucagon is ready to go.)

I have to be patient and wait for each meal
and pay close attention to just how I feel.

My body gives clues when I'm high or I'm low.
The device on my arm also helps us to know.

Alerts are set up
to alarm on our phones.
If I'm high for too long
we check for ketones.

Diabetes is work
from shots to blood samples.
But there's still time for fun.
There's lots of examples...

When I need exercise,
it's time for a run.
Bet you can't catch me!
Dad's too slow for his son.

At another event, my Teddy was sick.
I learned to treat him at the "Teddy Bear Clinic."

To help me become an athletic force
my favorite event had an obstacle course.

I swung high on a rope just like a real ninja.
Bet you thought I would fall. Be honest now, didn't ya?

I can play with my friends
and compete in all sports.

I can take insulin
and eat food of all sorts.

Andrew means *Warrior*
which I try to be.
Type 1 diabetes
will **not** define me.

This past year has taught me
to take things in stride:
to do what's required
while enjoying the ride.

It's not easy, nor hard.
It's just how I live.
One key to it all
is to stay **positive**.

I know more about diet
than most my age would.
Being used to a schedule
can only be good.

The pokes and the needles...
Yeah, sometimes they sting.
But I battle type 1
and can be **anything**!

One day, a great dad
is what I'd like to be.
Yet my dad says he
wants to be more **like me**.

I'll continue to learn
and continue to grow
with one whole year down
and a lifetime to go.

THANK
YOU FOR
LEAD
ING

 ANDREA

ISBN: 978-1-730-70349-2

Thank you to all of the teachers, nurses, doctors, friends, and family members that help make living with diabetes so much more manageable for Andrew.

Please do not treat any of the material in this book as a substitute for medical advice. Diabetes treatments vary from person to person.
If you have, or think you may have, diabetes, please consult with your own doctor for diagnosis and treatment information.

We love hearing from and interacting with our readers. Please feel free to:

 Like Us!   https://facebook.com/YearOneWithTypeOne

 Follow Us!   https://www.instagram.com/YearOneWithTypeOne

Follow Us!   https://twitter.com/YearOneTypeOne

 Feedback!   https://www.goodreads.com/book/show/43161042

E-mail Us!   YearOneWithTypeOne@gmail.com

https://www.owleyebooks.com

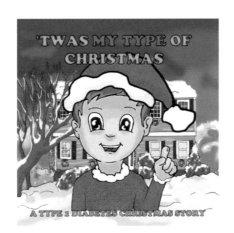

Made in United States
Cleveland, OH
22 October 2024

Some T1D groups like to host fun events. One time we all sat past the tall outfield fence